The Enchanted Forest

Chapter One

ONCE upon a time long ago in a land near the top of the world was a peaceful fishing village by the sea. Everyone who visited the village said how pretty it was. This was because of the beautiful wood carvings on all the buildings. In fact, all the buildings were built of wood, which made them very warm during the long cold winters.

THE ELVIN STORIES

By Bromley Coughlan
in collaboration with François Earp

illustrated by
18/1 Graphic Studio

AuthorHouse™ UK
1663 Liberty Drive
Bloomington, IN 47403 USA
www.authorhouse.co.uk
UK TFN: 0800 0148641 (Toll Free inside the UK)
UK Local: 02036 956322 (+44 20 3695 6322 from outside the UK)

Because of the dynamic nature of the Internet, any web addresses or links contained in this book may have changed since publication and may no longer be valid. The views expressed in this work are solely those of the author and do not necessarily reflect the views of the publisher, and the publisher hereby disclaims any responsibility for them.

Any people depicted in stock imagery provided by Getty Images are models, and such images are being used for illustrative purposes only.
Certain stock imagery © Getty Images.

This book is printed on acid-free paper.

ISBN: 978-1-7283-5423-1 (sc)
ISBN: 978-1-7283-5422-4 (e)

Print information available on the last page.

Published by AuthorHouse 07/28/2020

authorHOUSE®

The Elvin Stories

The people who lived in the village were unlike any other people. They had very slight bodies, but their hands and fingers were long and very strong, and their ears seemed to be pointed. The strength in their hands and fingers was due to chopping, sawing and carving wood from the trees in the large forest, which lay in-land near the village. The villagers all wore green clothes, dyed from the juice of the leaves from the forest.

Most of the villagers worked in the forest. They used the wood to make furniture, tools, bowls, plates, and even their knives and forks. Above all they liked to make toys for the children, and they sold these to the sailors on the ships that came to the village.

The people liked the trees and flowers that grew in the forest, as well as all the animals that lived there. They knew they must take care of the forest, because if they didn't there would be no wood in the future. So, they would only chop down a few trees, collecting branches of trees that fell to the forest floor, and re-using wood when they could.

The winters were so cold that the sea would start to freeze in the late autumn, and not melt until the following spring, when the ships would return. The villagers who did not work in the forest were fishermen, shopkeepers and some would look after their reindeer herds.

The reindeer were very important to the village during the winter. The reindeer would help villagers bring the wood from the forest on sleighs, as well as supply the village with milk.

The village was always a happy place.........until the Vikings came.

Chapter Two

One quiet and peaceful early spring morning after the sea-ice had melted the first sailors of the year arrived in the village. These sailors were like no other the villagers had seen before. Most were very tall and had long fair hair, and others had red hair. In the beginning they were like other visitors to the village, they were kind and in awe of all the beautiful wood carvings. The Vikings asked if they could trade with the villagers for lots of the toys, furniture and other beautiful things hand crafted by the villagers. The villagers said that they would gift to the Vikings some of what they asked for, but the Vikings wanted more. The villagers would only use fallen wood and not cut down the trees, so could not give the Vikings more. This angered the Vikings, but the villagers would not change their mind.

The next morning the villagers awoke to the sound of crying and screams, as the Vikings rounded up all the villagers into a large building. The Vikings told the villagers that they had to work for them otherwise the Vikings would set fire to the forest and take the reindeer away with them.

The villagers were put into groups, with some of the men taken into the forest each day to cut down trees, other men had to make ships and weapons for the Vikings. The women had to cook for the Vikings, who had enormous appetites, which meant that there was very little food for the villagers themselves.

The Vikings watched the villagers very carefully to make sure that none escaped, and that no villager was allowed into the forest in the dark. The only free time the villagers were given was a few hours on Sunday afternoons.

All through the spring and summer the villagers worked under the Vikings control, hoping that when the autumn arrived, the Vikings would leave the village. As the first ship was completed, it left the village with some of the Vikings and weapons. The villagers hoped the remaining Vikings would soon depart, but worse was to happen. The ship returned with two other boat loads of Vikings. Life became more miserable as there was even less food for the villagers.

Chapter Three

Elvin was a young villager. All the villagers were kind and generous, but Elvin was the kindest and most generous of them all. He worked in the forest, and he would always look forward to eating his lunch in a clearing, as the Vikings would be gorging themselves, and not worry if the villagers wandered a short distance away.

One day as Elvin was eating his lunch in a forest clearing, a hunched old man with much wrinkled skin stood in front of him. He was leaning on a staff much taller than him, and Elvin felt that without it the old man would fall over. Even though Elvin had very little food, he asked the old man if he would like to share his lunch. The old man nodded his head and ate as though he was starving, leaving almost nothing for Elvin. When he had finished the old man stood up and waved farewell before returning to the forest.

Every day after their first meeting the old man would appear in front of Elvin just as he was about to eat his lunch. Each day Elvin would ask the old man if he wanted to share his lunch. The old man would always nod his head, and never say a word to Elvin, before returning to the forest after lunch. Elvin began to wonder if the old man could not speak. Elvin noticed that each day the old man would eat slightly less than the day before, and the old man was growing taller, hardly needing to rely on his staff. After a month the old man ate hardly any of Elvin's food and was now taller than Elvin.

The days were becoming shorter with the work in the forest only possible for a few hours. It was during a lunch on a Friday towards the end of autumn that the old man spoke his first words to Elvin.

His voice was very assured and not like that of an old man. "The Vikings will never leave this place while you work for them."

Elvin was shocked by the old man's words "We have no choice" he replied.

"But they can't make you work, if they can't find you."

Elvin was confused and said so to the old man.

"On Sunday afternoon bring all the villagers to this clearing, and I will explain. It is important that everyone comes."

Elvin nodded his head, and when he looked up to speak to the old man again, he was nowhere to be seen.

Chapter Four

Elvin did not know what to do, and that evening he spoke to his father and mother about the old man. His mother told him to ignore what the old man had said, but his father asked Elvin to repeat his story many times. He would question Elvin in detail about the meetings with the old man. Every now and again a smile would flicker across his father's face, he was proud of his son.

His father took Elvin to meet the village elders in the village hall where he was asked to repeat his story again. He was asked to leave the hall while his father and the elders spoke more. It was after mid-night before his father returned to their home. Elvin was still awake when his father came to his bedside.

"It took a lot of persuasion, but the elders have agreed to gather all the villagers in the forest clearing on Sunday afternoon."

The next day word spread around the village about the gathering in the forest, and plans were made so that the Vikings would not notice that the entire village was meeting in the forest. It was usual for the Vikings to be sleepy on Sunday afternoons because they would eat a large lunch on Sundays.

Elvin found it difficult to sleep Saturday night. He worried that the Vikings would discover the plans, he worried the old man would not appear, he worried that what the old man had planned would not work, he worried that the villagers would not agree to the old man's plans. It was after mid-night before he eventually fell asleep.

Chapter Five

Sunday morning was like normal, it was the day when the villagers would normally do lots of cleaning and tidying, ready for a new week of work. Elvin's job on Sunday was to go to one of the workshops in the village where toys were made, and pick up any off-cuts of wood on the floor of the workshop, and this would be put with any of the toys that were not perfect. The men and women, who carved the toys during the week, would dismantle the imperfect toys and reshape the pieces, together with off cuts so nothing was wasted.

On Sundays the young men and women would be trained how to carve, using the wood from the imperfect toys and off-cuts. Elvin always looked forward to his carving lessons, but Elvin did not have the patience to carve the detail on the toys. Today was worse than usual as Elvin kept thinking of the afternoon meeting in the forest. After three mistakes he was asked to help elsewhere in the workshop.

As soon as he was finished at the workshop, Elvin left the village and made his way to the clearing in the forest to eat his lunch. The old man appeared in front of Elvin. He did not look like the person he saw in the clearing a month ago. He was taller, his skin less wrinkled, his eyes were brighter, and his clothes looked clean, and even his staff was straighter and as tall as the old man himself.

"The whole village agreed to meet you here this afternoon" Elvin said.

The old man merely nodded his head and he stood with Elvin waiting for the villagers. They did not have to wait long before the first people arrived. In less than half an hour every villager was in the clearing. The villagers were becoming nervous that the Vikings would discover the village was empty and come looking for them. The noise of the crowd was unsettling, and Elvin was concerned that people might start to return to the village. At that moment, the old man struck his staff on the ground and sparks flew from the top of his staff. This immediately silenced the crowd.

"If you want to be free of the Vikings listen very carefully to me." The old man's voice was clear and commanding. "None of you will return to the village tonight, and not again until the Vikings have left for good."

The crowd started murmuring and again the old man struck his staff on the ground, but with more force, and in addition to sparks flying the staff glowed yellow.

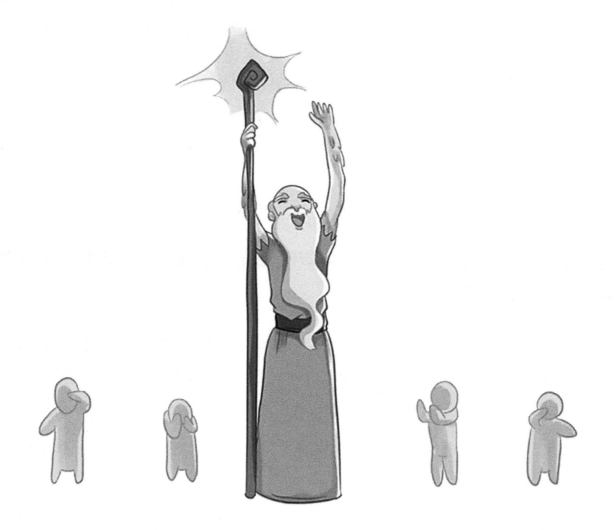

The old man spoke again, his voice louder with more authority "The Vikings will never leave while you are here to do as they command. So, you must leave...."

"But they will chase us and hunt us down" a voice in the crowd cried out.

"Only if they find you, and I can promise they will not find you if you agree to what I say."

The villagers were silenced and Elvin asked, "What should we do?"

The old man smiled at Elvin and replied "Many generations ago your ancestors lived in this forest, and you care for it very much. If the Vikings do not leave, the forest will die because they will want more and more weapons, furniture and ships. The trees will not be able to grow quickly enough to replace those that are chopped down to provide the wood for the Vikings. For one year from today, whenever you are within the forest you shall be invisible from the Vikings. In that time the Vikings will leave. I will give you an hour to consider what I have said."

The villagers immediately started to talk to each other, and after a short while, the elders of the village approached the old man "If we do agree, how can we feed ourselves and keep warm tonight?"

The old man smiled, "You can thank Elvin for his generosity." He struck his staff on the ground a third time and piles of food and furs appeared in the clearing "There is enough here to keep you clothed and fed until you can find food a shelter in the forest."

The elders returned to the crowd to convince everyone to live in the forest. During this time Elvin noticed that the old man was no longer in the clearing. Elvin went to look for his father and mother, and when he found them, he said "You knew who the old man was."

Elvin's father replied "I was not sure, but I believed him to be a powerful warlock, who inhabits the forest. No-one knows exactly where he lives, and now we probably know why."

Chapter Six

The first week was the most difficult. The villagers were nervous that they would be discovered by the Viking search parties. The Vikings searched the forest, but the days were short, and the light was not bright, and the villagers were careful to be very quiet and still when the Vikings were close.

The villagers quickly adapted to the forest and found enough food to last the winter as well as warm places to sleep.

After only a few weeks the search parties became less frequent, with the Vikings believing the villagers had fled further away from the village. As winter arrived there were no search parties at all.

Early the next spring the Vikings sent out search parties into the forest. The Vikings could be overheard, and they were angry and hungry, with no-one to provide them with food or goods to sell, and they were arguing with each other. From the highest tree in the forest the villagers could see the sea and would keep a look-out on watch.

A few weeks after the beginning of spring the look-out shouted that the Vikings' ships were leaving. There were no search parties in the forest, and a few days after the ships had left, one day at dusk a few villagers went to the village. It was a mess. The Vikings had destroyed most of the homes setting them on fire so there was nowhere for the villagers to live.

The small group of villagers who went to the village saw that there was one small ship still in the harbour, and that light was coming from only one building at the port. They returned to the forest taking nothing with them.

After another month the last remaining ship also departed. The villagers were careful to remain in the forest, in case the Vikings had left anyone behind to spy on them.

Chapter Seven

Spring quickly became summer, and then the leaves in the forest started falling to mark the beginning of autumn.

It was one year since the villagers met in the forest clearing. Once again, the whole village gathered at lunchtime, this time to celebrate that the Vikings had left their village.

Just as they started their meal the warlock appeared in the clearing "You are free of the Vikings, but I fear if you return to the village other people will come and try to control you. Your freedom depends upon you remaining in the forest, and I can keep you invisible if you stay within the forest's borders."

Elvin stood up and spoke to the warlock. "We have already spoken amongst ourselves and we do not wish to live outside the forest. But we do still want to make our toys for our children, and the children outside of the forest. We do not want anything for the toys other than the happiness it brings children at Christmas. Is there anything you can do to help us?"

"I will see what I can do" replied the warlock and he smiled.

Why Rudolph has a red nose

Chapter One

Many years ago, the reindeer Dasher, Dancer, Prancer, Vixen, Comet, Cupid, Donner and Blitzen would help to deliver the toys made of wood carved by the people who lived in the enchanted forest. Elvin was not very good at carving, so he would ride the sleigh when delivering the wooden toys.

Everyone believed that all the toys were delivered on one night, Christmas Eve, but this would be an impossible task. What actually happened was that Elvin and the reindeer would start their deliveries two weeks before Christmas Eve. The toys were carved from wood that could only be found in the enchanted forest. The warlock, a powerful magician had cast a spell, so that the wooden toys could not be seen until Christmas Day morning. The reindeer were born, and lived in the enchanted forest, and the sleigh pulled by the reindeer was also carved out of wood from the enchanted forest. The warlock was also able to enchant the reindeer and the sleigh, so most of the time they were invisible when making their deliveries. But sometimes late on Christmas Eve the enchantment would wear off, and often the sleigh being pulled by the reindeer could be seen. The people who saw Elvin called him Father Christmas.

Chapter Two

With so many deliveries to make Elvin would rotate the reindeer so that Dasher, Dancer, Prancer, Vixen, Comet, Cupid, Donner and Blitzen would not be exhausted before Christmas Day. The biggest time for the deliveries was Christmas Eve, and for such an important time Elvin would harness all the reindeer to the sleigh, so when some people saw the sleigh, they would see all the reindeer.

While the delivery of the wooden toys for Christmas was a very important task for Dasher, Dancer, Prancer, Vixen, Comet, Cupid, Donner and Blitzen they worked all through the year. These reindeer were chosen from the herd that lived in the enchanted forest. Only the strongest reindeer were picked to pull the sleigh. At other times Dasher, Dancer, Prancer, Vixen, Comet, Cupid, Donner and Blitzen would work alongside the other reindeer. Most of the younger reindeer all hoped that one day they would be chosen to pull the sleigh, but none dreamed of this more than Rudolph.

Rudolph was strong for his age, but he was not fully grown, so he would work all year round pulling large loads, hoping that it would help him to grow strong more quickly. He would always be the first to volunteer for any task and was prepared to take on additional work. Some of the other younger reindeer would sometimes make fun of Rudolph, but he would ignore their jokes and taunts, and just work harder.

Chapter Three

As more children were born, the demand for the beautiful wooden toys grew. Elvin realised that more deliveries were required so they needed more reindeer than Dasher, Dancer, Prancer, Vixen, Comet, Cupid, Donner and Blitzen. So, Elvin decided to try out other reindeer for the extra deliveries.

Rudolph was in the group of the new reindeer. Rudolph was still one year away from being fully grown, but his strength and willingness to work hard, meant that Elvin could not ignore him. Rudolph rose to the task, and despite being the youngest, within a few short days he became the natural leader of the new group of reindeer. Rudolph would pull harder than the other reindeer, and when one of the other reindeer tired and started to flag, Rudolph would encourage the reindeer through their tiredness.

Elvin was so impressed with Rudolph; he would sometimes give Rudolph more work and switch him with Dasher, Dancer, Prancer, Vixen, Comet, Cupid, Donner and Blixen. Rudolph did not fail Elvin's confidence and took the additional workload in his powerful stride.

Christmas Eve was only one day away, and despite the extra deliveries there were still a large number of toys to deliver. The sleigh was being loaded with more and more wooden toys and becoming heavier and heavier. To make sure all the remaining wooden toys were delivered on time, Elvin decided that they needed to start very early on Christmas Eve, so as soon as Dasher, Dancer, Prancer, Vixen, Comet, Cupid, Donner and Blitzen were awake they would start their final delivery before Christmas Day.

The reindeer were harnessed to the sleigh and Elvin shook the reins, but as hard as they tried the reindeer could not move the sleigh. Elvin called upon the other elves to give a push, hoping that once the sleigh started to move the reindeer would be able to pull the sleigh themselves. Everyone pulled and heaved but the sleigh would not move freely.

Some people wanted to take off some of the wooden toys, but Elvin explained that he did not want to disappoint any children on Christmas Day. Someone suggested that they needed extra reindeer. Elvin asked that the harness be extended so that one more reindeer would be able to pull the sleigh.

"Only one reindeer?" some asked.

To which Elvin replied "The reindeer I have in mind can pull like two other reindeer. Find Rudolph."

Rudolph was fast asleep after working the night before with the other new reindeer on what they thought was their last run, and he was unaware that the sleigh would not move. He woke up and saw the problem. Shaking himself fully awake he prepared himself for the task ahead of him.

The harness had been adapted to include Rudolph in front of the other reindeer. Elvin made sure that all the reindeer were braced against his reins when he shook the reins and shouted a loud "Yah."

The reindeer pulled and strained but still the sleigh would not move. Then Rudolph's nose flared large and he snorted, as though calling to the other reindeer to try harder. He rose with his two front hooves off the ground and appeared to jump forward. The sleigh moved, not far but it had certainly moved.

Encouraged by this, Elvin shouted again and once more Rudolph rose, but this time the other reindeer followed his lead. As they all jumped the sleigh started to gather momentum, and then they were off and running with the weight of the sleigh helping them to slide across the snow.

Chapter Four

Rudolph was so happy to be with Dasher, Dancer, Prancer, Vixen, Comet, Cupid, Donner and Blitzen on the most important delivery before Christmas Day.

They flew in the sky making all the stops required to ensure the children had their wooden toys. The problem was the enchantment that kept them hidden from view wore off more quickly than usual and more people saw the sleigh being pulled by the reindeer.

Elvin could hear the cheers and shouts of the happy people who saw them "Look there's Father Christmas with his reindeer, and the one in front has a red nose."

Elvin was amazed by the thought of a reindeer with a red nose. When the sleigh returned to the enchanted forest, Elvin jumped down and went to Rudolph and immediately saw that he did indeed have a red nose. At first Elvin was concerned that Rudolph had cut his nose, but Elvin did not find any blood. Then Elvin realised that the strain of trying to pull the heavy sleigh has caused Rudolph's red nose.

Elvin smiled "Rudolph you can be very proud of your red nose, you have earned your place with Dasher, Dancer, Prancer, Vixen, Comet, Cupid, Donner and Blitzen. Next year you will start with them, and we cannot make the sleigh too heavy, but with more and more children we are going to need more help."

So that's the story of why Rudolph has a red nose.

The boy who didn't believe in Father Christmas

Chapter One

A great many years passed since Elvin first started delivering wooden toys to the lands near the enchanted forest. More children were in the world and news of Father Christmas had spread and so the demand for toys had grown. Also, children's tastes changed, and while wooden toys were always a favourite, now there were requests for other types of toys.

The elves had to develop new skills, they still made as many toys as they could but sometimes it was just not possible to have access to all the raw materials, or the modern factories required to assemble some toys. So, the elves became the designers of toys, having the ideas of what children would like as a new toy, and the toy makers would give some toys to Father Christmas so he could deliver these to the children. Some years certain toys were very popular, and Father Christmas would simply just not have enough, so he might have to give the children other toys.

Elvin also had to change with the times. Everyone who lived in the enchanted forest wore green, and for many years, he would wear his normal clothes when he made his deliveries. More than a hundred years ago Elvin decided that he needed to wear something brighter, he wanted something that could be seen by the children who caught sight of him, and he chose a red coat and trousers with white fur on the collar and cuffs.

The reindeer were the descendants of Rudolph, Dasher, Dancer, Prancer, Vixen, Comet, Cupid, Donner and Blitzen. But even with the younger reindeer, they struggled to make all the deliveries. Elvin tried to make the sleigh go faster by fixing rockets to the sleigh. Even this was not enough, and so Elvin decided that he needed more help.

Chapter Two

Robert was six years old and he was the youngest of four boys. Robert didn't have many friends at school. It wasn't that he was unpopular, or bad at sport, it was just he enjoyed his own company. He liked to read books, newspapers, even the back of packets or boxes. After reading he would then ask questions. His mother, father and brothers were very patient with Robert's inquiring mind and would answer Robert's questions.

Robert loved school, and at weekends he would often try and find out more about the subjects he learned at school. His parents were very strict that Robert, and his brothers under the age of ten, were not allowed access to computers or mobile phones unless their parents or teachers were with them. So, Robert would ask his parents to take him to the public library.

The library was in the centre of town. One of his parents would take Robert to the library for an hour, if Robert would help them with any shopping they needed. Robert never complained about the shopping as he enjoyed all the different sights and sounds, and he was like a sponge soaking up facts as they walked around the centre of town.

One day Robert's father took him to one side and he gave Robert what looked like a book.

"This was my father's stamp album" Robert's father said as Robert opened the book.

From the first moment, he saw the brightly coloured pieces of paper, he was enthralled. Some were square, some oblong, and even some were triangles. Robert was very organised and would put each stamp on to the page for the country which issued the stamp. Every time he put a stamp on the page for the first time, Robert would look at a map, to see where the country was in the world.

Chapter Three

During the long warm summer Robert and his family went on holiday to a large house on a lake many miles from where he lived. It was a lovely house with a wood at the end of the garden. His father taught Robert how to fish. Robert enjoyed the quiet time while he fished, as he could read the books he brought from his home during the holiday.

Robert would always agree to make up the numbers with his brothers when they asked him to play ball, but his favourite game was when the whole family played paperchase. The first person would have a bag full of torn up pieces of newspaper, and that person would start running dropping the paper as he went, then the others would follow the paper trail. If the first person was caught before they returned to the house, then the chasers would win, if the first person returned without being caught by the chasers then they would win.

Robert's father made sure that everyone had a chance at not being caught, and the chasers would leave at different times after the first person had left the house. Robert loved to be chased. While his brothers, father and mother were much quicker than Robert, the delay before the chasers started made it much fairer. Robert was small and could squeeze through hedges and climb trees, and sometimes he would lay a false trail and then double back and take a different path. Robert found an old map in the house and would study it to plan to take different paths through the wood when it was his next turn to be chased.

The books were all well-thumbed by the time he returned home and he was looking forward to school starting after the holidays. He couldn't wait for his next visit to the library. The games of paperchase had made Robert stronger and he found that he had a love of running.

While on his holiday Robert bought a packet of stamps for his album, but these stamps were much older than those in his album and lots were from countries Robert could not find on his map. Robert's father explained they were from countries which had changed their name, or from countries that were now part of other countries. Robert wanted to visit the library where they had maps in an old atlas and he could find out more about the countries which issued the old stamps.

Chapter Four

In the new school term in the autumn, Robert enjoyed the new books he was asked to read. He also now enjoyed the nature lessons outside, when the weather was not cold or wet.

Robert was asked to take part in the end of term play, celebrating Christmas. Robert was asked to play one of Father Christmas' helpers, and when asking his parents if Father Christmas was real, he heard one of his brothers laugh behind their hands. His parents replied, "Of course he is," but for the first time he wasn't sure he believed them.

"Where does he live?" Robert asked.

"Lapland" his mother told him.

"I have never heard of it" Robert said.

"You will find it in one of the old atlases in the library" his father replied.

As the end of the term approached the weather became colder, and the days were becoming shorter, which meant going to school and coming home in the dark. It was a Saturday, only one week away from Christmas Day, and Robert's father had promised him a trip to the library. They tried to park their car in the usual place, but it was very busy, and they had to wait until someone left, before they could find a parking space.

By the time they had parked their car it was dusk, and as they walked towards the library it was very gloomy, and it felt like the evening. Also there were lots of people walking in the same direction, so they could not hurry along.

"Why are there so many people Daddy?" Robert asked.

"They are going to the area in front of the library for the turning on of the lights on the town's Christmas tree."

Robert was not pleased as it meant less time at the library, and he had just received a new pack of old stamps, which he wanted to put into his album. There were so many people that it wasn't possible to walk freely. Robert walked slowly with the crowd. Robert was being pushed, and he held his stamp album tight under his arm. There was shouting behind Robert, he turned around and saw a man dressed in a Father Christmas costume elbowing past the people behind him, saying "Excuse me I am late, please let me through." As the man came beside Robert his outfit caught the corner of Robert's stamp album, and it was pulled out of his hand. The stamp album fell out of Robert's hands onto the ground. He cried out "My stamp album!" He went to try and find the stamp album, but there were too many people behind him, and his father picked Robert up, so he did not fall over.

Robert and his father could not stop themselves from being moved along from where the stamp album fell out of Robert's hands. They moved to the edge of the crowd, then started looking for the stamp album. They hunted for two hours but could not find it anywhere. Robert's father tried to cheer him up "Don't worry Robert, Father Christmas will bring you a new one."

"I don't want a new one," Robert cried "and I don't believe in Father Christmas."

Chapter Five

Elvin had realised he needed more help to deliver all the presents on Christmas Eve. So, Elvin found people in each country to help him give out the toys. Those people would then find other people in each town to help, and in larger towns there would need to be more than one helper. These helpers would all wear the red costume like Elvin when Christmas approached, and so it would often appear that there was more than one Father Christmas.

The Monday after he lost his stamp album, Robert went back to school, but he found it difficult do on his lessons. He found himself thinking about his lost stamp album. When he was rehearsing the school play, Robert forgot his lines and had to be reminded by his teacher.

During his lessons on Tuesday morning the class were asked to write a letter to Father Christmas, describing what they would like as a Christmas present. Robert's sheet of paper was blank when the teacher walked round the classroom.

"Robert, you haven't written anything, is something wrong?" His teacher asked.

"I don't believe in Father Christmas." Robert's eyes were wet with tears.

His teacher knew about what happened the previous Saturday, and she pulled up a chair and sat beside him. "I am sorry about you losing your stamp album, but I am sure you will get a new one. Please write a letter, and maybe you will get a better stamp album."

After a little while Robert did what was asked of him, and he wrote the letter, but secretly, he thought that his parents would probably buy him a new album for Christmas.

Chapter Six

It was Christmas Eve afternoon, and after the school play it would be the holidays.

In the six days since Robert had lost his stamp album everyone had tried to lift his spirits, his family, his friends at school and his teachers. Towards the end of the week, he began to smile and he really enjoyed his outside nature lesson, even though it was snowing. They were looking at snowflakes and trying to see their different shapes before they melted. That reminded Robert about the different shapes of stamps. Robert believed he might be getting a lot of new stamps to replace those he lost the previous week.

His parents came to his school play, and Robert was word perfect. As a reward, Robert could choose the dinner of his choice, for Christmas Eve supper. He chose pizza and ice cream, which his parents and brothers loved, and they had lots of fun playing card games after supper.

Robert was very tired and fell asleep watching television. He could just remember his father carrying him into his bed, and his mother putting him into his pyjamas.

Robert's bedroom was at the top of the stairs. Suddenly he woke up with a start. He looked at the clock on his bedside cabinet, it showed '04:30'. He put on his dressing gown, and quietly crept downstairs, so as not to wake anyone else.

He walked to where the Christmas tree was, and underneath he saw a pile of presents. Robert searched the gifts with his name on, and the largest parcel was in the shape of a box bigger than his stamp album. He thought about going back to bed, but he wanted to see what was in the box, and he quietly opened the present so as not to make any noise.

Robert was very happy, it was a stamp album, and one which had the names of the countries of today, and of yesteryear. There were packets of stamps, for Robert's new stamp album both old and new. Also, in the box was a book explaining where the stamps came from. Then there was a noise behind Robert.

"Hello, Robert. I hope I didn't wake you, but I am very pleased to meet you."

Robert turned around, and there was an old man with white hair, in a red suit. "Who are you?" Robert asked.

"I think you know," the old man replied, "my name is Elvin."

"I don't know who that is."

The old man smiled, "Some people call me Father Christmas."

"I don't believe in Father Christmas; I must be asleep dreaming." Robert said.

"Oh, well you might be, but I believe this is yours." The old man held Robert's stamp album in his hands. "One of my helpers accidently knocked it out of your arms. He picked it up but couldn't give it back to you. When you said you didn't believe in Father Christmas I had to come and see you in person."

The old man walked over to Robert and handed him the album. Robert opened the album and saw his stamps that he had carefully placed on the pages. He looked up towards where the old man had been standing, but he was nowhere to be seen. There was a flash of light outside the window, and Robert ran over to look outside. There was Elvin on a sleigh with reindeer pulling it across the newly laid snow. Suddenly the rockets fired and the sleigh rose into the sky.

Robert waved to Elvin, "Yes, I do believe in Father Christmas, and now I have two stamp albums."